Moby Stink

BOOK 3

By CHRIS RUMBLE

TRICYCLE PRESS
Berkeley/Toronto

For Cathy, my partner in adventure!

Tricycle Press
an imprint of Ten Speed Press
PO Box 7123
Berkeley, California 94707
www.tenspeed.com

Design by Chloe Rawlins based on a design by Betsy Stromberg
The illustrations in this book were rendered in pen and ink.

Library of Congress Cataloging-in-Publication Data

Rumble, Chris, 1961-
  Moby stink / by Chris Rumble.
      p. cm. — (The adventures of Uncle Stinky ; bk. 3)
  Summary: With some help from his nephews Zack and Billy, Uncle Stinky lands
a famous catfish, recalls how a restaurant became the haunt of zombie chickens,
and foils the plot of a madman.
  ISBN-13: 978-1-58246-145-8 / ISBN-10: 1-58246-145-7
  [1. Adventure and adventurers—Fiction. 2. Humorous stories.] I. Title.
  PZ7.R88765Mob 2005
  [Fic]—dc22
                                       2004030091

Paperback ISBN 1-58246-145-7
First Tricycle Press printing, 2005
Printed in the U.S.A.
2 3 4 5 6 – 12 11 10 09 08

Contents

Episode 5: A Fishin' Mission with Evil Opposition

"Call me Stinky. Everyone does. Some years ago my momma an' daddy gave me the name. Personally, I don't smell anything, but most folks say I stink like onions an' old fish.

"Now, I'm no expert on onions, but I do know a thing or two about old fish. I have spent my share o' time down at the fishin' hole. Whenever I find myself feelin' a little low, when a cold, bitin' wind chills my soul, it is then that my heart longs to set out fer the open waters."

Good, morning, Unk! We're ready!

"I see ya got on your lucky fishin' hat!"

Yep.

"What's up with Billy?"

Oh . . . he said he's gonna be the bait. It's pretty smart when you think about it: What could drive a catfish crazier than a big *mousefish*?

Ya got your secret weapons ready, Unk?

"Been workin' on 'em for two whole weeks!"

I *thought* you were puttin' out a bit more stink than usual, because I had to tighten up my clothespin a couple of notches.

"It's gonna get even stinkier when the sun comes out in full force. But just remember, Zack: what's stinky to *you* is *downright irresistible* to Ol' Whiskers!"

And that's how our adventures began the morning of the 238th Annual Catfish Rodeo and Fish Fry. Every year on the Saturday closest to the April full moon, the entire town of Hootenholler makes its way out to the middle of Lake Ookarotcha and gathers on Nomanzan Island. Hootenhollerans come with every kind of fishing gadget imaginable, each hoping to be the one who finally snags the biggest catfish of them all, Ol' Whiskers.

LAKE OOKAROTCHA

Home of OLDS ROCK and the ANNUAL CATFISH RODEO!

1. CRIMEA RIVER
2. STINKY'S COVE
3. WUZZAT SOUND
4. BEDDABEE SHORE
5. IYAMM SHORE
6. NOMANZAN ISLAND
7. OLDS ROCK
8. HOOTENHOLLER SEWER SYSTEM PIPELINE
9. BROWN LAGOON
10. "CREATURES" FROM THE BROWN LAGOON
11. WODZUPP DOCK
12. DAWN KIER COVE

LAKE OOKAROTCHA TRIVIA... When you look at it a certain way from Lou DeLoop's crop dusting plane, Lake Ookarotcha looks like an angry donkey with a REALLY, REALLY LARGE HEAD.

"Now, Ol' Whiskers has been frustratin' an' flusterin' an' flabbergastin' fishermen forever. Tales of his preposterous proportions an' the many ways he has kept from gittin' nabbed have been passed down through the generations, reachin' all the way back to Hootenholler's prehistoric days ...."

DINOSAURS tried to hook him.

He confounded CAVEMEN.

OOK OOK DOOKA

TRANSLATION: "GOLLY GEE, OL' WHISKERS SURE IS ONE LARGE FISH. I HAVE A DREAM OF CATCHING HIM ONE DAY ..."

The ancient EGYPTIANS worshiped him as a god.

THOUGH OL' WHISKERS DID NOT MERIT A "GREAT PYRAMID," THEY DID BUILD HIM A "MEDIOCRE CYLINDER."

COLUMBUS CAN HAVE CREDIT FOR THE "NEW WORLD." WHO CARES?! JUST GIVE ME OL' WHISKERS!

VIKING BUBBA ERIKSEN found his way to Lake Ookarotcha.

COLONIAL DAYS: Before the Revolution, Patrick Henry had other passions.

GIVE ME OL' WHISKERS OR GIVE ME DEATH!

SOME BELIEVE THAT OL' WHISKERS, LIKE BIG FOOT OR THE LOCH NESS MONSTER, IS MOSTLY LEGEND AND WILL NEVER BE CAUGHT!!

There's always lots of excitement over the Catfish Rodeo. But this year, an Ol' Whiskers sighting had folks worked up into a real catfishing frenzy. The

Thursday before the rodeo, Mikey Little came running into town all wide-eyed, yelling, "I saw him jump! I saw him jump!" When asked how big Ol' Whiskers is, he said, "Bigger 'n Wendell."

Further adding to the Catfish Rodeo fever was the impressive lineup of contestants.

All of Hootenholler had been buzzing since word got out that we'd have a celebrity joining our tournament: Barry Cooter, cable television personality and host of the wildly popular fishing show, *Hook 'Em an' Cook 'Em*. Mr. Cooter made a big entrance in his fish-shaped helicopter, the *Whopper Chopper*.

No fishing tournament would be complete without Red Wiggler, Hootenholler's all-around fishing champion. Uncle Stinky has a special talent for bringing in catfish, but Red can catch anything that swims. When asked to reveal his secret, he simply answers, "I got worms." After he says that, most folks just back off and leave him alone.

"Sheriff Frank Yavelot, Principal Delores Tenchen, and Deputy Doug Stine took their reg'lar spots in the judges' booth at the foot o' Olds Rock.

"*Anyhoo*, Mayor Naise, rock-namer extraordinaire, kicked off the festivities with his traditional words o' well-wishin' to all the fishermen an' fisherwomen."

"OLDS ROCK"

OFFICIAL NAME: "OLDSMOBILE ROCK"

The brainchild o' Mayor Samuel Naise, namin' the rock was his first order o' business durin' his first term. He told the City Council that the folks up there in Massachusetts had a real famous rock that attracted a heap o' tourists. He said if we follered their example and named our rock after a car manufacturer, we'd get lots o' tourists, too. The Council heartily agreed. ✱

So, oldsmobile Rock stands as our answer to their Plymouth Rock.

And we think our rock is far more impressive, by the way. We sent our very own Clyde Swampnoggin up yonder to get a gander at their highfalutin' so-called celebrity boulder. He said he didn't see what all the fuss was about. Accordin' to him, it's barely a pebble compared to ours. So there.

✱ HISTORIAN'S NOTE: AFTER THIS EARLY SUCCESS, TO THE CITY COUNCIL'S DISMAY, MAYOR NAISE KIND OF "GOT STUCK" AND SPENT THE BULK OF HIS FIRST TWO YEARS AS MAYOR NAMING VARIOUS ROCKS AROUND TOWN, RESULTING IN THE "TOUR OF ROCKS"

"Greetings, fair citizens! Welcome to the 238th Annual Catfish Rodeo and Fish Fry! I'm sure each and every one of you is ready for some *fooracious,* but friendly, competition. As always, we will *bestoo* upon the angler who lands the biggest fish the usual array of prizes: a half dozen eggs from Wendell's Eggs-N-

Things, white or brown, your choice…

"…a month's supply o' doorknobs from the Door Knob Store…

"…a free toenail clipping from Sweet Tootie's Roadside Toenail Clipping Parlor and Petting Zoo…

"…plus, Tootie promises to let you pet the possum!"

15

"Suddenly, the Mayor was silent, which was very unusual, so it got everybody's attention.

"With every eye glued on him, Mayor Naise pulled a sack o' somethin' from his coat pocket, held it up, and said in a volume borderin' on hollerin':

"'We want to make this year's competition a bit more *intertriguing*. I hold in my hand a fresh sack of boiled peanuts delivered from Stan's Stand just this morning.'

"Then, with great dramatic flair, he strutted around, wavin' them peanuts in the air like the circus master he always wanted to be. Prancin' over to the bait shack door, he pulled a staple gun out of his other coat pocket.

"With a great KA-CHUNK that echoed across the still waters of Lake Ookarotcha, he

stapled them salty delights high up on the door.

"All of Hootenholler stared at the sack o' succulent snacks, lickin' their lips, longin' fer a sample o' them nuts. Mayor Naise continued:

"'These gourmet *deliciacacies* will be awarded to the *fortunicious* fisherman who *ensnaptures* Ol' Whiskers. Bring him in and you'll get the peanuts ... and we'll all have the most *gigantuous* fish fry in history!'"

With the prize package sweetened beyond their wildest dreams, the contestants stampeded to their boats. Barry Cooter led the charge.

He boarded the *Pink Wad* and roared out from the dock, stirring up a huge wake that tumped over poor Mrs. Capoochowl's boat. He looped back around, leaned over the starboard bow, shook a huge harpoon in her face, and yelled:

"The Catfish Rodeo was kickin' into high gear! As usual, I enjoyed fishin' in my own little private corner o' Lake Ookarotcha. Other fishermen have to worry about lotsa folks comin' around, scarin' off the fish, but not me. I had plenty o' elbow room to put my secret weapons to work.

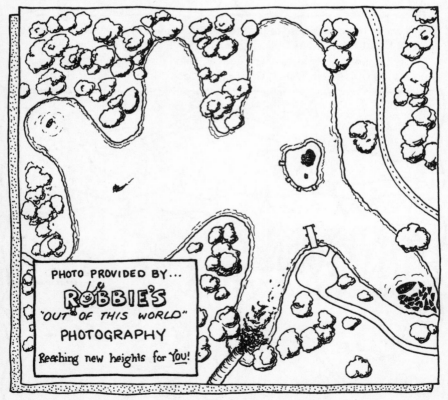

22

"On the other side o' the lake was an entirely different scene. Most folks figgered Barry knew what he was doin', so, in spite o' his warnin', they follered the *Pink Wad* as closely as possible, in hopes of snaggin' Ol' Whiskers. This made Cooter madder 'n a wet hen.

"What nobody understood at the time was that ol' Barry had a bone to pick with Whiskers."

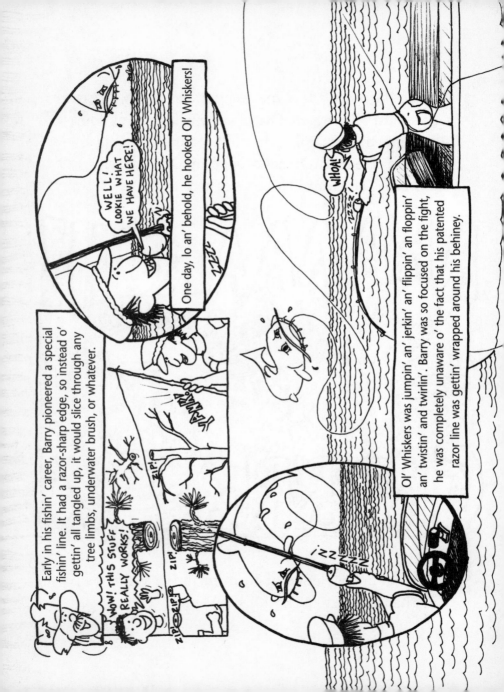

It wasn't long before the catfish were leaping and splashing all around us. On the far side of the lake, the other contestants continued to fight over the "best spot." But the fish would have nothing to do with any other bait but Stinky's.

Meanwhile, Uncle Stinky waited patiently for his pellets to work their wonders. As he has told me many times: "The secret, Zack, is to never give up doin' the thing you know to be right, an' bein' willin' to wait, no matter how long it takes, for the *magic*." So, while the other folks were fretting and fussing and fighting over who was going to catch the next big fish...

...Stinky was sitting peacefully, flinging out his line and pulling it back in, flinging out his line and pulling it back in, in a steady rhythm that seemed to be in harmony with the endless supply of ripples that circled out from our boat, connecting us to the rest of the world. But then...

Ol' Whiskers exploded out
of the water! Everything seemed
to slow down as he sailed high
above us. Billy and I stood up in the
boat, taking it all in. But ol' Stinky
remained at rest, keeping that same
rhythm with his cane pole.

Then Whiskers completed his dive on the other side of our boat, slipping into the water, hardly making a splash at all. And he was gone.

Uncle Stinky flung his line out one more time, then froze. For the first time he lowered his pole. His eyes widened.

Whiskers was airborne again, this time coming from the rear. His mouth was open wide in a huge grin, his eyes locked on Uncle Stinky as he headed downward.

Stinky grabbed us and shouted,

The big fish gobbled up just about every Pit Pellet in Stinky's bucket. Then *the magic happened.*

For the first time in his long life, Ol' Whiskers was caught.

He got wedged into the hull of our boat and couldn't get out. But you know what? He didn't seem to mind at all ... as long as Stinky kept feeding him the extra pellets he had ripening in his left armpit.

"I kept ploppin' them pellets into Ol' Whiskers's mouth while Zack an' Billy straddled his tail an' paddled us back around to the judges' booth. As my overloaded boat pulled out from the cove an' into the middle of Lake Ookarotcha where we could be seen, the other contestants dropped their fishin' poles out o' sheer shock. Risin' above the gasps was one bloodcurdlin' scream.

"I guess ol' Barry was a teeeny bit upset over not winnin'.

"Everybody knew the rodeo was officially over. Mayor Naise whistled an' waved everybody back to Nomanzan and hollered, 'Fire up the grill, boys! We're all gonna satisfy our *varoocious* appetites for catfish and take home doggie bags, too!'

"He handed me my prize package and barked at Wendell, 'Crank up your chain saw, Egg Man, so Stinky can start cutting the catfish filets!'

"The chain saw roared, and the fish-fryin' portion of the festivities was under way!

"The Hootenhollerans' hankerin' for catfish was even more powerful than their pinin' for peanuts. Ready to gorge themselves, they gathered 'round the gargantuan grill built generations ago in faith that Ol' Whiskers would one day be delivered to them. As the flames flew upwards, the crowd moved in an' out an' around the big broiler in a way that reminded me of a tribal ceremony I saw once on one o' them there National Geographical *dockermentaries*.

"They hoisted a humongous fryin' pan over their heads and headed down the hill. Ol' Whiskers looked up at me, knowin' it was finally his turn to be rolled in the batter.

"I slipped one last pellet between his curlin' lips an' said, 'You *really do* like these itty-bitty bread balls, don'tcha, boy?' He let out a sigh, savorin' what would be his last meal. I felt a flutterin' in my gut over what I knew was about to happen to Whiskers. I leaned over, rubbed his head, looked into the legend's eyes, an' whispered, 'I wish I had some more pellets for ya, but I'm all out. So, close your eyes and brace yourself, ol' cat, 'cause I gotta put this chain saw to work.'

"Now, ya cain't be wimpy when ya run a chain saw. So, I let off the choke an' ran it wide open. As I revved it up, the hungry Hootenhollerans drummed on that big ol' pan an' chanted,

"Okay, I admit it: I *was* enjoyin' their adoration a little. The blue-gray smoke of burnin' oil billered from the chain saw's hot-runnin' engine. The freshly sharpened blades turned at top speed, reflecting the orange light of the nearby flames.

"I was swingin' that chain saw 'round like one o' them samurai fellers. Then, in one smooth jujitsu kind o' move, I made the first cut.

"And, just like that, the pieces of what used to be my boat floated away, an' Ol' Whiskers slipped into the water."

Hootenholler's One of a Kind and Unique

TOUR OF ROCKS

Featuring ROCKS named by the Honorable Mayor Samuel Naise.

STOP #1

THE MAJESTIC OLDSMOBILE ROCK

STOP #2

THE HARD ROCK

The Hard Rock is Hootenholler's largest flint outcropping. Folks come from all over to tap their teeth on it just to see how hard it really is. Ronald Emeet sets up his food warmers on a picnic table and sells Tuna Helper to the visitors. He likes to keep it interesting, so, on Wednesdays Mr. Emeet serves Squirrel Helper. But Fridays are his favorite, when he makes up a big pot of "Betcha-Can't-Guess-What's-Bein'-Helped." He calls his little business the "Hard Rock Cafeteria."

Now, on to stop #3. This rock looks like two of our residents. On one side, it looks like Chip B. Von Toast, the cook down at the "Eat Here and Get Gas" Grill and Filling Station. From the opposite angle, it looks like Walter Wahlkarpit. Since it looks like both Chip and Walter, Mayor Naise named it "The Rock of Chip-Walter."

STOP #3

EASTERN VIEW   WESTERN VIEW

"CHIP"   "WALTER"

Rock #4 juts up out of the middle of Norman Clature's hog waller. (A warning to our guests: While visiting this stop on the tour, please don't irritate the hogs by dumping half-eaten portions of Squirrel Helper into the waller, making socially unacceptable noises while clearing your nasal passages, or forcing your political views on them.) Actually, this formation is two separate rocks, and when you pretend that the mud is the ocean, they look like a whale coming out of the water. Mayor Naise named this popular attraction "Norman's Rock Whale."

STOP #4

40

At stop #5 you'll see a collection of 36 little rocks, all of which look amazingly similar. You can see them in a fancy display case in the lobby of Ray Diosiddy's Movie Hall.

STOP #5

THE ROCK-ETTS

To remind folks of the attraction, Ray lets one of his sons pull the little glass case in his wagon so the Rock-etts can appear in the Thanksgiving Day Parade each year.

STOP #6

Our next rock is found in Nelson Fernbucket's backyard. On this famous rock, you will find the names of local men written in Magic Marker. These are the names of men whom Nelson himself has determined to be "all-around fine fellers." A name can be added at any time he sees fit, so folks like to visit regularly to see if any new fellers have earned a spot on the boulder. Nelson didn't know what to call the rock, so he appealed to Mayor Naise, who named it "Nelson's Rock of Fellers."

JIMMY STAN
FRANK DORSEY
STINKY ZACK
HOLLIS SAMUEL

The last stop of our tour is Wendell Rock. The City Council told Wendell that it looks like two eggs lying on the ground. That's their story and they are sticking to it.

STOP #7

WENDELL ROCK

HOOTEN HOLLER'S
TOUR OF ROCKS

It's both one of a kind AND UNIQUE!

If you liked the "Tour of Potholes and Other
Modern Geologic Formations" over there in
Tater Ridge, you'll be downright slaphappy
over our Tour of Rocks.

Make your reservation today by calling City Hall at
555-HOOT. If he's not playing checkers, Mayor Naise
will be happy to show you where the rocks are.

Admission: 50 CENTS per person or TWO for a DOLLAR!

This is a walking tour. However, if you choose
to take the self-guided version, you can run,
hop, skip, or do the cha-cha from site to
site-what do we care?

Buy ONE WASHTUB of TUNA HELPER for $24.95,
get the SECOND WASHTUB at HALF PRICE!

(Dine-in only.
No sharing or take-out boxes.)

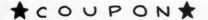

Get 10% OFF on SQUIRREL HELPER when you
BRING YOUR OWN SQUIRREL. (Coupon must
be presented with squirrel. Please make sure
squirrel is really dead before presenting.)

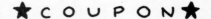

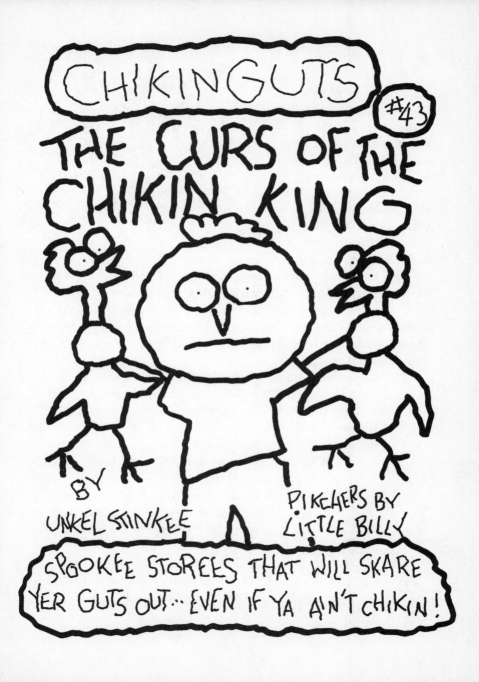

Not far from here, off ol' Scraggly Branch Road, there stands an abandoned chicken farm an' restaurant.

Now, do what ya want, but I suggest you stay far, far away from there 'cause the place is real old an' about to cave in on itself. And, well...it's just not a safe place fer young'uns.

And then there are the tales surroundin' it: Tales of creepy cluckin' noises, black eggs with nothin' but a musty dust inside 'em, an' people goin' in an' comin' out thinkin' they're chickens...or not comin' out at all. Some folks say only a fool would darken the door 'cause it's haunted or under some kinda crazy chicken curse.

I'm still not sure about all that, but when I's a young'un, me an' Frank an' Sam an' Wendell an' a buncha other boys all joined the Little Rangers. We were proud to wear the badge of Little Ranger Troop #43.

One weekend, we went campin' up yonder in Wart-Nosed Willy's Woods. On a dare, we went hikin' down Scraggly Branch Road.

Havin' not been used in years, the road was overrun by trees and brush. In some spots, we had to walk single file.

Oh, yeah...an' to prove how brave we were, we went at night. With no flashlights.

We'd barely started our hike, when outta nowhere, clouds filled the sky, blockin' what little bit o' light the moon was givin' us. Then, we started hearin' what sounded like scratchin': Scraaaatch...scratch, scratch...scraaaaatch.

Our fearless leader, Master Ranger Martin Friar, said it was most likely just branches blowin' and scrapin' up against one another.

We kept movin', feelin' our way through the darkness.

We came to a clearin' an', lo an' behold, there it was: a dark silhouette of the main house o' the old chicken farm. A big gust o' wind came rushin' through an' that rickety ol' house moaned an' groaned.

Then, we heard what could best be described as peckin'.

Peck...peck, peck...peck...peck.

The scratchin' and peckin' grew louder. We strained our eyes, tryin' to see. I got this sick feelin' in my gut an' goose pimples popped up all over my body. I said, "Let's go back." Wendell sneered at me: "Huh-huh-huh! Don't be a chickun."

Scratch, scratch, scraaaatch.

Peck...peck, peck.

Peck, peck...PECK!

"OUCH!"

Mr. Friar was holdin' his ankle an' hollerin', "Run, boys! Run! Get outta here!"

We all tried to skedaddle at once. We tripped over one another, but then scrambled to our feet. Branches slapped us in the face and briars grabbed our Little Ranger pants as we ran through the darkness.

About a mile down the road, we stopped to catch our breath. We couldn't hear any scratchin' or peckin', so we felt a little safer. I looked around an' took a head count.

"Where's Mr. Friar?"

"I thought he was right behind us," Frank said.

Then Wendell said, "I's tryin' ta run an' slammed inta him, but he just stood there, like he's in a trance or sump'n. Then I tripped on them zombie chickuns."

"Zombie chickens?"

"Yeah. They had no feathers, an' they felt dead-cold. Their heads hung limp like they necks was broke but they's still walkin' an' cluckin'. Last I saw o' Friar, he's surrounded by them zombies an' walkin' with 'em up to that old house up there."

We ran back to Hootenholler an' told our folks what happened. They all chuckled at what a hilarious joke Mr. Friar had pulled on us.

When four days passed with no sign o' Mr. Friar, they weren't laughin' anymore. Six weeks went by an' neither hide nor hair of our leader was found, and folks began to figger he was never gonna be found. On April 3rd they called off the search...an' shut down Troop #43.

Strangely enough, on the very day (4/3) they gave up on him and shut us down, Martin Friar would have turned 43. All them 4-3s seemed like a sign to us. So, that night, all of us ex-Little Rangers made a pinky swear. On the night of our own 43rd birthday, each of us would honor Mr. Friar by returning to Scraggly Branch Road, to the very spot where we last saw him.

Before I go on, I need to take ya back to where all this started.

Ya see, way back in the mid-1800s, Scraggly Branch Road was a main thoroughfare through these parts. It was just a narrow dirt road, but if ya wanted to go to Tater Ridge ya had to go by way of Scraggly Branch 'cause it was the only way 'round Mulebone Mountain.

About halfway 'round the mountain, there was a busy intersection where Possum Skull Drive dead-ends into Scraggly Branch. That intersection became a hub of activity an' that's where Morris "Mo" Beakman built his "Chicken King" empire an' made his fortune.

Folks would come from all over to buy an' sell chickens. Bein' an astute businessman, Mo opened a restaurant for the hungry travelers. He called it "This Is Your Plucky Day."

Ya see, Mo let the chickens run all over the place so customers could eyeball 'em fer themselves. This is what made his place so different. When the customers saw the chicken they wanted, they'd get up, chase it down, wring its neck, an' then pluck it right there at their table. That might not sound so good to you, but it was loads o' fun fer them old-timey folks. They liked to see who could pluck the fastest an' cleanest an' do the fanciest neck-wringin'. Every day, a new Chicken Pluckin' Champion would be declared. Mo even let the folks keep the feathers fer pillows.

When his empire was at its height, Mo would boast that he was cookin' one hunnerd an' twenty-six chickens every day. He threw his whole life into his chicken dynasty. So much so, he never slowed down enough to raise a family of his own. I guess, in a way, he saw the reg'lar customers as his family. An' so it went—for over twenty years, Mo enjoyed his reign as the Chicken King.

Then, the government came in an' built the new Tater Ridge Highway. Instead o' goin' around Mulebone Mountain, they took dyney-mite an' blew a passage right through the middle of it. When the wide, two-lane road was done, ever'body loved it 'cause you could be in Tater Ridge in three hours instead o' nine.

An' Morris Beakman, the Chicken King, was cut off from his customers. No one wanted to use a bumpity, dusty road like Scraggly Branch. Besides, since ya could git to Tater Ridge so quick, there was no need to stop to eat.

On the day they opened the Tater Ridge Highway, Mo had 943 chickens scratchin' an' cluckin' an' peckin' all over the place an' zero customers. Though he didn't know it yet, on that day, Mo lost everything.

As the story goes, he stood like a statue for hours at the front window, starin' at the empty parkin' lot while nearly a thousand chickens ran roughshod over the restaurant. The hours turned into days. With each passin' day, the chickens grew wilder, fightin' over a dwindlin' food supply, peckin' one another an' peckin' Mo. But Mo remained motion-less, starin' into the emptiness.

By day nine, a few screws had come loose in Mo's head. He started mumblin', "I am the Chicken King. I am the Chicken King. I am the Chicken King."

By day twelve, he was shoutin' at the chickens, "I AM LORD OF THE CHICKENS! BOW BEFORE ME!"

Of course, chickens don't speak English an' don't know how to bow, so they jus' kept cluckin' an' scratchin'...an' peckin'.

On the seventeenth day, Mo went berserk, chasin' chickens down an' wringin' their necks an' pluckin' 'em. He was a wild man. He growled an' grunted an' snarled an' snorted an' made other noises human bein's in their right mind don't normally make. And the feathers flew.

Mr. Beakman did not stop until he had plucked all 943 o' them chickens. They lay all over the place, featherless an' lifeless.

He stood in the middle o' the moonlit room, starin' at the limp chicken he had just plucked. As the clock struck midnight,

he ate the chicken...
the whole thing...
raw...
head first...
bones an' all.

Chicken blood trickled from the corner of his mouth as he squatted down in the middle o' the room, covered in feathers, exhausted an' alone. His mind now completely gone, he began to cluck.

He sat there for three days, cluckin'. By the end o' the third day, the chickens were gettin' good an' rotten. Around twilight, Mo began to feel like the chickens had been more of a family to him than anyone. Then, using all the authority he could muster as the Chicken King, he commanded the chickens to return to him. He called to them over an' over until his throat was raw. As the light of the full moon crept across the room, one by one, them rotten chickens started standin' up.

Mo grinned for the first time in days as they started scraaaatch-scratch-scraatchin' an' peck-peck-peckin'.

Mo stretched out his arms an' the chicken zombies gathered 'round their King...

...an' pecked him to death.

Well, yesterday I turned 43.

Even though other Little Rangers have turned 43 before me, to my knowledge not one o' them has gone back to honor Martin Friar.

Now, I've never broken a pinky swear, so just a little after sunset, I went.

I made my way up Scraggly Branch Road an' stood there in front o' that house, on the very spot where I last saw Mr. Friar holdin' his ankle an' hollerin' at us to run. I don't mind tellin' ya that I's scared, but a man's gotta do what a man's gotta do.

My quiverin' voice broke the silence: "Uh…thank you, uh, Mr. Friar for takin' care of us an' bein' a…great Master Ranger."

The words hung in the night and echoed off the walls o' the old place.

Then a howlin' wind kicked up an' all the hairs on the back o' my neck stood up. My duty done, I turned tail an' ran. You would have, too.

Safe at home, I locked my door an' hid my head under the covers.

But memories of Mr. Friar, Troop #43, an' all that happened that night raced through my brain. I couldn't stop thinkin' about the Chicken King gone mad an' zombie chickens peckin' out their revenge. My poundin' heart finally began to slow down a bit an' I slipped into a deep, but troubled, sleep.

In my dreams, I heard that scraaaatch-scratch-scratchin' and the peck-peck-peckin'. Zombie chickens climbed up on my

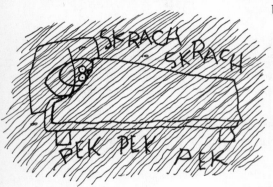

bed an' pulled the cover off me and started peckin' me all over. I tried to sit up, but it was like I was glued to my bed.

Then I saw Mr. Friar, covered in feathers, standin' over me and glarin' at me. He raised one o' them zombie chickens up over his head an' began to cluck: "Buck-buck-buckaaaawwww! Buck-buck-buckaaaawwww!" Still holdin' that zombie chicken way up high, he reached down and put his other hand on my chest. I just knew that this nightmare would end with Mr. Friar rippin' out my still-beatin' heart!

I tried to get up but couldn't move. I opened my mouth to scream, but nothin' came out.

Daylight finally did come, an' none too soon.

Thankful fer the chance to put all the spookiness behind me, I jumped outta bed an' headed for town, still wearin' the same clothes from the night before. I softly whistled "Sweet Home, Hootenholler." At the Corn Flake Café, I enjoyed a nice bowl o' corn flakes. As I slurped down the last drop o' milk an' wiped my chin, I reached into my vest pocket for the usual 39 cents. A shock wave ran up my spine as my hand felt somethin' metal—somethin' way bigger 'n a quarter—an' strangely cold.

I pulled it outta my pocket an' my heart skipped a beat.

It was one of our old Little Ranger badges.

I slowly turned it over, holdin' my breath.

On the back it read:

Episode 6: A Villain Willin' to Do a Little Killin'

Okay, Billy. We're ready. Go ahead.

 Uhngyah-Yah-Yah-Yaaaaaaaaahh!!

Good. A little louder and a lot more irritating, and add the tongue waggling thing.

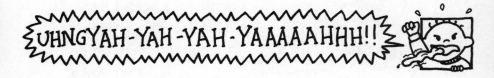

UHNGYAH-YAH-YAH-YAAAAAHHH!!

Great! You've almost got it! Give it one more shot. This time, add that high-pitched whiney sound and make your eyes bug out like you did last night.

UHNGYANH-YANH-YANH-YAAANHH!!!!

Perfect. I can hardly tell the differ-
ence between you and Mr. Cooter!

For those of you who weren't
there, Billy is demonstrating what
Barry Cooter's screams sounded like as
he circled Nomanzan Island. As we stood staring at him,
he let the chopper settle into a hover just above our
heads and then he erupted like a volcano:

"Twenty years!
Twenty long years I have
waited! For twenty years,
every time
I sat down,
every time
I passed the
buns in the
bread aisle at the grocery
store, every time I went to the—well,
every time I sat down—I have been reminded of the
soft, cushiony tush that was once mine. I *know* that that
fish—that *freak of nature*—ate my hiney.

58

"I have seen it in my dreams. He still carries it, hiding it from me in his tremendous tummy, teasing me and taunting me, daring me to come and get it. And *today* was the day I was going to gut him and retrieve the rump that is rightfully mine.

"As I suspected you might, you bumbling idiots got in my way. You robbed me of the revenge I have yearned for all these years. Well, never again! I have worked long and hard preparing for your removal—installing massive underwater hydraulics systems, perfecting the Ginsu net, genetically engineering the *barakillers*, all the while conscientiously maintaining immaculate dental hygiene, a point that has absolutely no bearing on my deep-seated need to avenge my loss but thought you'd find interesting nonetheless.

"Anyway, soon you will be out of my way forever and I will be free to face my fanny-filled foe. HAR-HAR-HAR-HAAAAAAARRRRR!"

As the volume of the *Whopper Chopper* fell, a steel wall rose. It came up out of the still waters of Lake Ookarotcha and surrounded us. The beautiful scenery that met our eyes only moments before was now completely blocked from our view.

Then, with a few clicks and a zip, a net emerged from one side of the wall and spread to the other.

Tinky gut.

Uncle Stinky's GUT (Gauge of Unseen Trouble) kicked into high gear. He picked up a stick and threw it into the net.

We watched as the stick was sliced into little pieces and knew immediately that the net was made of Barry's razor line. Nomanzan Island was our prison.

The dying fire crackled as we stood there in stunned silence. Uncle Stinky turned around and tried to comfort the crowd:

"Wendell's wailin' got everybody all worked up, an' out o' fear they tried to run away. But since we was on an island, all they could do was run in a circle."

The docks creaked as they sank, pulling our boats under with them. We could see the worry on Stinky's face. He looked at me and said:

CWEEEAK!

"I know there's a way outta this, but we're not gonna get anywhere until we stop the panic. Let's think for a minute, Zack. The net is made of razor-sharp line, right?"

"Right."

"But it's still made of nylon ..."

"And nylon melts!"

"Right you are, Little Buddy! Stoke the fire, folks! We got a razor net to melt!"

"The words were barely outta my mouth an' K.C. was karate choppin' into little bits any dry wood she laid eyes on. She reduced the bait shack to splinters in short order! I had to duck an' roll off the steps to keep from gettin' chopped myself!

"Hootenhollerans were haulin' wood almost as fast as she could chop, which is sayin' somethin'. In no time, the fire was blazin' again. The flames flew up above Cooter's wall an' that ol' net shrunk back like it was nothin'!

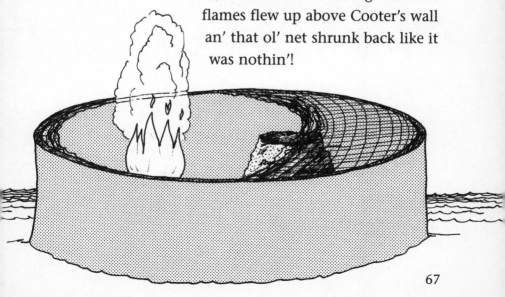

"We were risin' to the challenge, but Nomanzan Island was still sinkin'! I got a sick feelin' in my innards when I heard the *Whopper Chopper* come roarin' back with Crazy Cooter. He was not happy about his net.

"Cooter opened a trapdoor an' out spewed about 327 o' the biggest, hungriest *barrycuders* you ever laid eyes on. Addin' to the fear factor, they's the jumpin'est fish ya ever did see. They had that water churned up like one o' them turbo washin' machines down at the Soap Opera All-Nite Laundromat an' Karaoke Lounge.

WHIRRRRR

SOAP OPERA KARAOKE SONGS
- **Puttin' on the Rinse**
- **We Got Bubbles** (Right Here in River City)
- **I'm Too Sudsy for My Shirt**
- **Time for Me to Dry**
- **Wisk and Shout**
- **I'll Be Washing You**
- **Long Black Stain**
- **The "Momma Washed the Colors with the Whites and Now All My Underwear is Pink" Blues**
  AND MORE!

"Now, I'll grant ya, this was not the most encouragin' development of the day. But folks lost all perspective quicker 'n lickety-split. They went into another one o' their runnin' fits. Only this time they had less room to work with. With the island sinkin' an' all, the circle they were runnin' in was quite a bit smaller. So much so, that folks in the middle o' Nomanzan were just kind o' spinnin' on one leg."

SOAP OPERA
KARAOKE
KING

HOW TO EXPRESS PANIC WHEN THERE IS NO ROOM TO RUN...

Keep left arm by your side.

Keep left leg stiff.

Shift body weight to left heel.

Push off with right leg.

For full effect frown and open mouth wide.

Finally, BUG YOUR EYES for the finishing touch!

Pump right arm like there's NO TOMORROW!

SPIN IN A CIRCLE!

Grabbyerpose!

Uncle Stinky was waving his arms and shouting, "Stop yer runnin'... an' yer spinnin'...an' grab yer poles! We got a lotta fishin' to do!"

But they didn't stop. Stinky sighed a big, frustrated sigh. I looked at him and said, "You're gonna have to sweeten the pot to stop 'em this time, Unk!"

He reached into his back pocket, pulled out one of his gift certificates, held it up, and hollered, "Whoever catches the most *barrycuders* gets a free toenail clippin' at Sweet Tootie's!"

Even though a large number of folks in our town have grossly overgrown toenails, they kept right on runnin'...an' spinnin' too, of course. That is, until Uncle Stinky played his trump card: "And don't forget— you get to pet the possum."

Mikey, who has better-than-average toenails, spoke up:

"Most of us still have our poles, Uncle Stinky, but all of our bait went down with our boats."

Red Wiggler smiled and chimed in: "Don'tcha worry none, Mikey. I got 'nuff bait fer ever'body. I always have plenty o' bait!"

Dr. Delores Tenchen asked, "What do you mean, Red? Your tackle box is on the lake bottom with your boat, like everyone else's. And, I might add, anything that might have remained in the bait shack has long since been consumed by the fire."

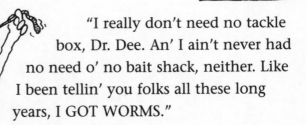

"I really don't need no tackle box, Dr. Dee. An' I ain't never had no need o' no bait shack, neither. Like I been tellin' you folks all these long years, I GOT WORMS."

"Usin' both hands in rapid-fire fashion, Red started yankin' worms out from places too gross to mention. Normally, only about half o' the folks in Hootenholler would be willin' to touch Red's worms. But I guess the danger o' gettin' dead an' the possibility o' pettin' the possum will motivate Hootenhollerans to do just about anything.

"So they went to fishin'. They was bringin' them *barrycuders* in left an' right. As fast as they could jerk 'em outta the water, K.C. an' her friends would chop 'em on the head. With one mind-blowin' motion, these karate-choppin' champs would knock 'em out cold, unhook 'em, an' send 'em sailin' into the fire. It was a sight to behold: a town wide display of expert fishin', barbecuin', an' the ancient martial arts. Thankfully, the "Hook 'Em an' Cook 'Em" cameras were still rollin', so it was captured on film for the whole world to witness.

"We knew that every last *barrycuder* had been caught, 'cause the water got real still again. In all the excitement, no one thought to keep up with who caught the most, so my Sweet Tootie's gift certificate was still up for grabs. But Sweet Tootie said that if we ever got outta this mess she'd give everybody a turn at pettin' the possum.

Natcherly, folks got all excited an' they was huggin' an' high-fivin' one another, when we heard the *Whopper Chopper* crossin' the lake again."

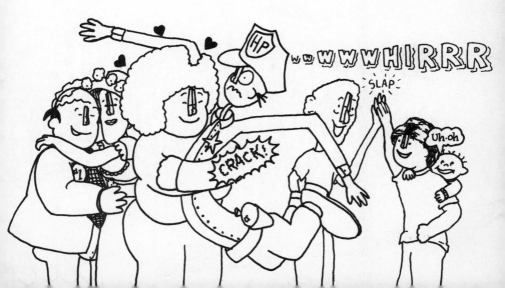

Mr. Cooter engaged some kind of autopilot. He left the cockpit, threw open the side doors, and crawled up on the harpoon gun mounted on the main deck.

"Alright, so you melted my Ginsu net and charbroiled my *barrakillers*. You must be very proud of yourselves.

WELL, NOW THAT YOU MENTION IT, WE DO FEEL A FAIR AMOUNT OF PRIDE AND ACCOMPLISHMENT. IT'S KIND OF YOU TO NOTICE, MR. COOTER.

"AAARGH! You blockheaded boobs! In spite of your hometown heroics and all of the heartwarming 'we-can-do-anything-if-we-all-work-together' nonsense, Noman-zan Island is *still* sinking. From this moment on, anyone who tries anything that remotely resembles swimming or scaling the wall will be harpooned like a human shish kebab."

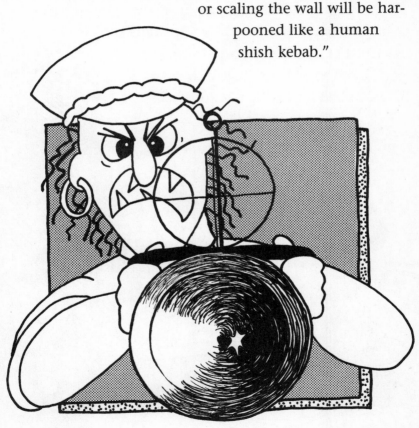

"Well, as you prob'ly guessed, them poor, frightened folks went to panickin' again. But by this time the island had sunk so far, their runnin' fit had to be downgraded to a hoppin'-in-place fit.

Actually, there wasn't even enough room to hop, so what they wound up havin' is best described as a jigglin'-up-an'-down fit.

"In danger o' bein' jiggled to death, Billy climbed to the top o' Olds Rock.

"Then, inspiration whopped me upside the head! We could *still* buy a

little more time. The huge fryin' pan intended for Ol' Whiskers was just barely stickin' outta the water. If only for a little while, it could be our lifeboat.

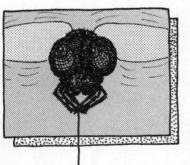

"Another vision o' hope flashed before my eyes. One o' my flies flew up an' bumped into my nose, danglin' one last pit pellet. He hovered there, starin' at me, as if awaitin' my orders.

"I jutted my chin out a little, looked square into my buzzin' buddy's amazin' compound eyes, an' whispered,

GO!

Uncle Stinky yelled, "Grab that skillet, people. We ain't dead yet!" and we lifted the frying pan out of the mud.

Stinky called out: "All together now! Put the pan on top o' Olds Rock!"

We surprised ourselves at how easily we pulled that gigantic skillet out of the lake and up over our heads. In a heartbeat, it was on top of the rock like it was made to be there.

WHIRR

Everyone continued following Unk's commands: "Now, everybody in, little ones first! You keep

it steady, Granddaddy, until everyone's in safe!"

Even though the water was just about over most of our heads, Granddaddy Longleggs was still bone-dry from the knees up.

"Dear ol' Granddaddy kept that pan from teeterin' until the whole town was evenly distributed across its black iron bottom. Those closest to Granddaddy helped pull him up an' in with the rest of us. He didn't wanna take up more 'n his share o' the room, so he just let his legs dangle over the side.

"Thinkin' nothin' of it, Granddaddy kicked the water a teeny bit an' made a few tiny splishy-splashes. Well, when he did that, ol' Cooter exploded!

DEAD MEAT!

RRRRRR

NOW YOU'VE DONE IT, OLD MAN! What you're doing definitely, albeit remotely, resembles SWIMMIN'!

HAR-HAR-HAR-HAR-HAR-HAR-HARPOON!

WHIRRRR-TIME!

"That nasty ol' Cooter jumped back behind his harpoon and pulled back hard on the triggerin' mechanism. With a CLANK, the harpoon was released from the barrel. But, just in the nick o' time, BoBo, Wendell, and Mrs. Filbert had put together their own show of force!

"As the *Whopper Chopper* made another orbit around Nomanzan, Cooter reeled in the harpoon to get ready for another crack at Granddaddy. Those manning the chickens pulled 'em back for reloadin'. Unfortunately, Wendell had put *all* o' his eggs in the first ammo basket.

An' Mrs. Filbert had donated all o' her doorknobs, too. Well, all 'cept for one. She reached deep into her sweatpants pocket an' pulled out the doorknob her grandma had given her on her seventh birthday. She stared at it all sentimental-like, then handed it over to Sheriff Frank.

"Frank loaded his chicken, pulled it with all his might, an' let her fly! His aim was true, but Mrs. Filbert's dearest doorknob simply bounced off o' the *Whopper Chopper* with a pitiful 'PING.'

"Cooter har-har-harred as he made another round.

"The harpoon rattled back in place as the waters of lovely Lake Ookarotcha began to trickle in an' fill the fryin' pan.

HAR! HAR! HAR!

I'M GETTIN' WET HERE DEPUTY DARLIN'?! ARE YOU GONNA SAVE ME OR WHAT?!?

ALRIGHT FOLKS, GET READY TO STAND UP!

"We were about to go under, but that wasn't enough for Barry. He was still determined to turn somebody into a human shish-kebaber. Knowin' we were outta ammo, he hovered right in front o' my good-as-gold granddaddy.

"As he pulled the trigger, all of our friends in the fryin' pan surged to shield Grand-daddy from the hurtlin' harpoon."

Then, *the magic happened!*

89

"No longer in danger o' bein' skewered by Cooter's harpoon, we treaded water an' celebrated an' held on to each other a little tighter. We'd come this far, an' we knew, no matter how long it took, we could take care o' one another until somebody found us.

"Billy dog-paddled over an' wrapped his little arms around my neck an' gave me a wet peck on the cheek. Zack was right behind him.

"We floated there together for a little bit. I looked an' saw my fly hoverin' just above the wall, still danglin' that pellet. Then…

"Ol' Whiskers sailed high above the wall. He was smilin' as he did a couple o' acrobatic flips! He joined us, announcin' his arrival with a humongous splash!

"He floated on the surface an' gave folks plenty o' time to warm up to him. Then, takin' three of us at a time, he escorted everybody safely over the wall an' back to the beautiful banks of Lake Ookarotcha."

Chris Rumble is also known as the "Reading Guitar Man!"
He visits schools all across the country getting kids all FIRED UP
about READING and WRITING! He wants to bring his
READING PEP RALLY and WRITING WORKSHOPS to your school!

Here is what some kids just like you said after the show . . .

"That was fun. Actually, it was FUNNY fun!"
—3rd grade boy

"That was more fun than playing Nintendo!"
—4th grade boy

"Uncle Stinky rocks!"
—5th grade boy

"I want to be a writer."
—5th grade girl

"I used to not like to read, but now that you encouraged me, I do."
—4th grade girl

"That story about Buford was so funny my head almost popped off!"
—3rd grade girl

"Would you sign my napkin?"
—4th grade girl

"You look like Garth Brooks."
—3rd grade boy

Tell your teacher or librarian to visit CHRISRUMBLE.COM
for more information!

HEY ALL YOU PICKLE FANS!

Have you seen Pickle "laying low" all throughout Uncle Stinky's adventures, or has he been too sneaky for ya? He appears a whopping 33 times in this book! See if you can find him on pages 8, 10, 13, 14, 16, 19, 21, 23, 25, 26, 28, 31, 32, 35, 37, 59, 61, 62, 65, 66, 69, 70, 72, 74, 76, 78, 80, 82, 84, 87, 88, 91, 92.

The Good, the Bad, and the Smelly
ISBN: 978-1-58246-122-9

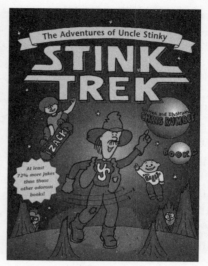

Stink Trek
ISBN: 978-1-58246-123-6

Hey kids! Don't miss a single one of Uncle Stinky's adventures.

Visit your local bookstore, or www.tricyclepress.com.